Cosy Burrow Books

VALKYRIE ACADEMY DRAGON ALLIANCE
Book Nine

BESIEGED

I0594621

"The dark elves are invading Asgard, and without help, the Valkyries will lose the battle. Fighters and dragons are falling left and right, and Kara the wingless Valkyrie calls upon an unlikely ally." Susie D. Proofreader, Red Adept Editing

Valkyrie Academy Dragon Alliance Books

Marked (Prequel)
Chosen
Vanished
Scorned
Inflicted
Empowered
Ambushed
Warned
Abducted
Besieged
Deceived

Cosy Burrow Books

VALKYRIE ACADEMY DRAGON ALLIANCE

BESIEGED

KATRINA COPE

any, and all, resemblance to actual persons alive or dead
or locations or events is entirely coincidental.
Published by Cosy Burrow Books

ISBN: 978-0-6486613-8-2

Michael ~ your support means the world to me

Through this link you can sign up for my newsletter and receive a FREE copy of Marked plus updates about my fantasy books, sales and notification of giveaways.

- CHAPTER ONE -

W*hat?* Anger laces Elan's voice. *Loki is behind all this?*

"Calm down, Elan." I pet her under a scale just before the saddle. "I know it sounds bad, but we don't know what he's really up to."

She swerves abruptly and changes direction.

"Where are we going?" I ask her.

I'm going to visit Mother, of course.

I sigh deeply. I'm going to be in more trouble with Mistress Sigrun for not going back to the Valkyrie Academy straight away. But I'm always in trouble, so it's not going to make that much difference either way, and the dragons need to get some answers.

I'm sure Mother would like to know what's going on, Elan says.

"You're right. I expected as much. There's a lot of explaining to do, and there's still more I need to uncover, but I know you dragons deserve an answer." I pull my hand back and hang on to the straps with both hands. "I know I'd be pretty upset if I were in your position and someone was stealing my babies."

Hours pass, and the chilly breeze bites into my skin. I pull out my dragon-scale cloak, wrap it around me, and yank the hood over my head. I haven't been to the dragon wastelands since Elan was rescuing me from Odin, and it wasn't a welcoming reception. This memory nibbles at my thoughts, and I worry my bottom lip, although I know a lot has changed since then.

During our flight, the landscape slowly changes. The dragon wastelands are different from the academy area. The terrain is rugged, and the temperature is hot—almost the opposite of the land of the giants, the area in which the dwarf giants are keeping their dragons.

Even though the air had warmed, I continue wearing the dragon-scale coat, hoping it will help me to blend into Elan's back. I hope this will keep the other dragons from being alerted to a Valkyrie entering their territory. I learned the hard way last time that they don't take kindly to Valkyries on their turf. Even though Elan is the second in charge of these dragons because she is Eingana's daughter, this didn't stop an angry and emotional dragon from wanting to attack Elan and eat me, despite the risk of severe punishment.

Elan descends onto the spot where I stayed for nearly a week last time I was in the wastelands. Sobek lands on the mountaintop not long after and stands in front of Elan.

Elan. His eyes rise to me and tighten. *And Kara. He bows his head as though showing respect.*

Elan squats on the ground. I remove my cloak and tuck it into the saddle's pouch before swinging my leg over her back and sliding down her side. "Sobek. It's been so long."

He nods and wraps his wing around me briefly in a one-armed hug.

Even though Elan has grown since I was here last, Sobek is still bigger. His shoulders are broader, and he looks more intimidating. If I hadn't met him previously, I would probably be quite scared in his presence. Instead, I stand firm as he bends down and sniffs me.

I reach out and touch his nose. "It's nice to see you again, Sobek."

I hear you have been through much since we last saw each other. He snorts, and warm air surrounds me.

"Just a few challenges. Nothing too bad."

Elan rolls her eyes. *You can't help but get yourself into trouble.*

I grin at her. "Just trying to keep you entertained."

Sobek fixes solemn eyes on Elan. *Why are you here, Elan?*

I'm looking for Mother. Have you seen her?

He nods toward the cliff. *She's down in the valley, sorting out an argument.*

Elan snorts out steam and dons an annoyed look. She stomps over to the edge of the cliff and looks over the valley. Her eyes focus on one spot, and she lets out an enormous roar. The noise echoes through the valley and across its fields.

I sneak up and peer from behind one of her legs. Several dragon heads turn up toward the mountain face, and I spot Eingana in the middle of all the dragons, her golden scales glimmering in the sun. She snarls at a couple of dragons then abruptly stops and turns to look up at the cliff face. As if in a final warning, she turns around and snaps at the dragons she previously snarled at then pushes off and flies up to the top of the mountain to greet us. The ground shakes briefly under her pressure.

Kara. She looks at me then turns to Elan. *Daughter.* Her eyes tighten. *What is the meaning of this? You are endangering Kara's life again.*

Elan spins and heads to the center of the mountain plateau, and I walk with her, attempting to remain under her large form, hiding from any prying dragon eyes in the sky. It is a lesson I learned from my brief stay in the dragon wastelands when I was in hiding from Odin and his punishment, a threat still fresh in my mind. I am a Valkyrie and an enemy to the majority of dragons. Elan halts in the middle of the plateau, waiting for her mother to arrive.

Eingana's heavy footsteps make the mountainside under my feet quiver, and the vibrations ripple up my body.

When she stops, Elan addresses her mother in a snappy voice. *There is a good meaning for this, Mother.*

Don't take that tone with me, Daughter. You know that it's too risky to bring Kara to the wastelands.

Sorry, Mother. Elan bows her head briefly, showing her respect, then continues her argument. *But there is a good reason that I have brought her here. Please do not take my tone as defiance. I am too distracted by the worries circling in my head. There are matters at play that weigh heavily on my mind, taking my focus away from showing you the respect you deserve.*

Eingana lifts her head and glares down at her daughter over the bridge of her nose. I cringe under Elan's body and absentmindedly back away a couple of steps. Eingana has certainly mastered an intimidating stare.

After a moment, Eingana nods. *Then tell me what weighs on your mind.*

Elan sits on her haunches and nudges me forward gently with her front leg toward Eingana. *I have brought Kara here to explain it.*

Eingana's curious eyes shift from Elan and focus on me. *Kara, what's going on?*

I swallow, but the lump doesn't move from my throat. The news I have will not be pleasing to Eingana. At one point, this dragon was very intimidating toward me, and the authority reeks from her. She is the leader of the dragons and one not to be messed with, although I've been through a lot to prove myself to the dragons. I'm glad that her attitude has softened toward me, considering she was initially going to eat me. The only reason she didn't was because I saved her daughter.

It takes a great deal of effort to remind myself that Eingana is concerned for my safety. I bow my head then stare up into her giant brown eyes. "I'm not sure it's as bad as what

Elan is making it out to be, but there is information that you should know. I do not know the full extent of what it means, so I don't want you to stress yet, and I don't want you to act inappropriately. At least wait until you know the full story behind it. I'm not sure myself. Please know that I don't in any way support this, and I don't know their intentions."

Oh, dragon scales, Kara! Get on with it. Can't you see that Mother is getting impatient? Elan waves a wing toward her mother. *If you don't hurry up and spit it out, then I'll say it. You know that my opinion is very biased.*

I sigh. "Yes, Elan. I'm getting to it. I'm trying to stop her doing exactly what you're doing."

Yes, I realize that. Elan sounds as if she is speaking through gritted teeth. *But he doesn't deserve your protection.*

"Maybe he does, Elan." I walk farther in front of her, spin to face her, and throw my arms out to the side. "Maybe he does deserve my protection because he gave me magic."

And that's a good thing, is it? Elan asks. *Because all it seems to have done is bring you grief.*

"But it also let me protect my friends and the other Valkyries from the invasion of the dark elves. It even helped me protect you."

That may be so, but the scum has also stolen dragon eggs. Elan is almost yelling.

Who? Eingana cuts into our argument, her voice thunderous.

I sigh deeply. This isn't how I wanted the information to come out.

- CHAPTER TWO -

Eingana's face is distraught and full of rage.

Who? Who is stealing the dragon eggs? I thought the zmey was the one taking the dragon eggs.

I wave my hands in a repeated, calming manner. "Just settle, Eingana." I make sure my voice is filled with respect so I don't poke the angry dragon. "Yes. The zmey is stealing the dragon eggs. But I found out the zmey is someone in particular."

What do you mean, 'someone'? Isn't it a creature?

"Yes. It is a creature. But the creature is a shape-shifter, and that shape-shifter is a someone," I say, keeping my voice calm and purposefully exposing the truth slowly, hoping she will calm down a little.

Eingana shakes her head and looks confused. *I don't understand.*

"The zmey is one of Loki's shapes," I say slowly and distinctly.

What? That traitor! Eingana stomps her foot, and the ground vibrates under my feet again, sending shivers down my spine.

I hold up a hand, palm out, motioning for her to stop. "But I have seen the dragons from the eggs, and he isn't harming them."

What do you mean? Eingana's voice thunders. *Why would he be stealing them if he isn't eating them?*

I shake my head. "He's definitely not eating them. They are healthy and seem well cared for."

Then what does he want them for? And why didn't he ask us or tell us where they are? We've been worried about these dragon eggs. We thought they had been eaten or sold on the black market.

"He has been stealing them for an army."

An army? Why would he need our dragons for an army? Eingana's expression is hard to read, and I'm unable to tell if she is upset or not.

I observe her from under a raised eyebrow. "I believe dragons can defend and attack naturally. Fighting a war would be second nature to you. You are a big and nasty breed when you want to be. The numbers he has will give them a very good chance."

How many dragons does he have? Sobek asks, nudging his massive form into the circle to join the conversation.

I gaze at each dragon in turn. "Don't you know?"

We've lost count over the years, Eingana says.

"Okay," I say slowly, pacing underneath Elan's shadow. I tap my finger on my lips. "There has to be at least sixty of them."

What? Eingana shrieks, pure anger seething in her eyes. *That is ridiculous. How could we have let sixty dragon eggs get stolen?*

I shrug. "I don't know, but you are talking about Loki. He is a trickster and very sneaky. I'm finding that out the hard way. I'm not completely sure if I can trust him. What I do know is that the dragons he holds are well cared for."

The leader of the dragons huffs, and steam shoots out of her nostrils, barely missing me. *That still doesn't take away from the fact that he's stolen them from us and didn't bother asking for them.*

"Would you have let him have them if he did ask?"

Probably not. We have lost enough eggs and enough babies. Our population is just stabilized but not enough for more eggs to disappear. If he takes any more, our community will diminish.

"They are still alive, so the dragon population hasn't diminished. Whether those dragons will remember you or treat you as part of their family, I don't know. But I have seen them firsthand, and I can vouch that they are healthy."

The scales on Eingana's forehead push together as she frowns. *How did you see them firsthand?*

"Loki changed into a frost giant, kidnapped me, and dragged me into Jotunheim."

The anger in Eingana's eyes transforms into worry. *To the land of the giants? How strange. Is that where they are?*

I nod. "Yes. The dragons are training there with dwarf giants as their riders."

The leader of the dragons huffs out another plume of steam.

I step out of the way. "Before you get upset, I think you should talk to Loki first. As I said,

I've seen the dragons firsthand, and they look very healthy and cared for. I'm just not sure of Loki's intentions with an army or if he ever plans on reintroducing them to their families."

Eingana continues to look peeved as she stomps around the mountaintop. She gazes at Elan over her shoulder. *I understand why you brought her here now. You're right. I'm sorry I judged you. This is crucial information.*

Elan bowed her head, casting her eyes to Eingana's feet.

Eingana stops in front of me, dropping her nose to stare into my eyes. *How long have you known?*

Her eyes feel as though they are piercing into my soul, and my heart flutters with apprehension. The guilt stirs in my stomach. I didn't come running to the dragons straight away, and now they are about to find out my betrayal. I want to back up and hide behind Elan's legs, but I remain firm, fixed to the spot.

I lift my chin. "I've had suspicions for some time now."

Anger starts to burn in her eyes, and they sharpen.

I hold up a hand. "I wanted to make sure my information was right before I came to you with this and destroyed all hopes of any alliance. I didn't want to wreck your relationship with Loki, especially with him being your negotiator and translator for Odin."

You could have given us some warning so we could be warier. She nudges her nose closer.

My feet remain fixed on the ground. I don't dare step backward. "As I said, I really didn't want a full-scale war against Loki. I still think you should discuss this with him now that you know. I don't know the full story. That way, you can come up with your own conclusion on whether you can trust him or not. Maybe he has all the right intentions and is having the dragons trained for the right cause."

Isn't taking them to the land of the giants and building an army there enough suspicion that he could be using the army against Asgard? If he's doing this for Asgard, he should be training them on Asgard, Eingana says.

"I understand where you're coming from. It does look bad. But he swore to me that he was using them to protect Asgard. Loki was building up an army because Odin is so pigheaded and not willing to listen, and also because Odin doesn't pay any attention to beings like me, who have Asgard's best interests at heart."

Odin is a goof. Eingana pulls her face slightly away from me, making her seem less intimidating. *But I still don't like it.*

"I'm hoping we can work this out together, peacefully, until we know what Loki's real intentions are. Then we can deal with it if he does have the wrong intentions."

Eingana paces, and her scales push together on her forehead. After several minutes, she stops and stands in front of me.

I guess you're right. I don't like it. But it's best to find out the full story, not that we can trust Loki, because he hasn't told us this whole time that he's the one stealing our eggs. But for the sake of Asgard and the rest of the dragons, we will have to play this safe and slowly find out more. In the meantime, we should start preparing our dragons in the wastelands to become an army.

"Aren't you natural fighters?" I ask.

We are rather vicious, yes. But we are not trained in combat. If Loki is getting these dragons trained, they may not have any sympathy for any other dragons. They may be wired to cut out all emotions and attack whatever. This won't be good for our dragons unless we do the same. At the moment, if these dragons find their babies opposing them in an army, I don't know how they will react. Even though it has been years of eggs stolen, some of these dragons still pine over their lost babies. She stomps her foot hard on the ground. *I can't believe that we did not see this before. I cannot believe that Loki has deceived us purposely. I'm not happy about this.*

"I didn't think you would be. But please remember, Loki has taken me under his wing for some reason. He helped protect me and marked me with magic, giving me a special ability. Before, I was wingless and gifted with nothing. He has done all of this under the disguise of one of his shapes. I have used this magic to protect dragons and to protect Asgard. So even though he has gone about this the wrong way, please hear him out and work at the truth behind it before you attack him."

Eingana stomps her front feet a couple more times then slaps her backside down on the ground in a sitting position. *I guess I don't have a choice. In the meantime, I will be training these dragons to fight. I don't like this, and I would like to take back control.*

- CHAPTER THREE -

I spend the night in the wastelands, taking shelter in the cave I used last time I stayed under the protection of Elan's family. It has been a long day, and the sun has already disappeared for the night.

The next day, silence overpowers the trip back to the academy, with both Elan and me lost in our thoughts. I hope I haven't stirred up a hornet's nest, but I can't hold back the information from the dragons. They regard Loki with so much trust in their discussions with Odin, and it's best that they know what they're dealing with. My stomach swirls with worry.

As for Loki telling me to withhold the information from them, I couldn't. The dragons have always been honest with me. Loki, on the other hand, has been deceptive and devious the whole way through.

We land in front of the academy, and Hildr, Eir, and Britta run up to us. Elan squats down, and after tucking my coat into the saddle pocket, I kick my heels over her back and slide down the side.

Eir's face is a beacon of concern. "Oh, Kara! We've been worried sick about you."

"Yeah. We've been waiting here for ages." Hildr plays with the hilt of her sword, a habit I've seen her do many times when she is nervous.

"Where did Mistress Sigrun send you?" Britta asks.

"She exchanged me for some souls to the angels of death and Freya. They took me to Folkvanger."

Hildr's eyes widen. "What?"

I nod. "I don't know if it was Mistress Sigrun's intended outcome. She probably expected them to harm me in some way." My brow puckers into a frown. "I don't know how many souls they traded me for. Even so, I'm not sure that it was worth it to them. All Freya wanted was to talk and find out if I knew any information."

"That's odd," Britta says. "The leader of the angels of death only wanted to talk with you?"

I nod. "I know, weird. But she didn't harm me in any way. Surprisingly, she is rather peaceful, considering the relationship we have with the angels of death."

Eir smiles wistfully. "I like the sound of her."

"Yes. I thought you would. Freya seems to think that I'm the peaceful one, but I mentioned that you're the peaceful one. You're always pining on peace and understanding."

Eir smiles. "You're not exactly violent, either. I know your heart is in the right place, so she's not completely off with her assumption."

Hildr frowns at Eir and me then crosses her arms over her chest. "So, what did she want? It's a lot of effort to go through just to meet up with you. There must be a more important reason."

"Apparently, she's heard about me and what I've been doing. I mentioned that you were all involved also and that it wasn't just me."

Hildr repetitively taps her foot. "And?"

"She wanted to know if I knew anything about another army."

Hildr stops her tapping. "Do you mean like the dark elves that invaded Asgard?"

"That's what I thought at first. But it's not what Freya meant. She's talking about another army based in Jotunheim."

Hildr scoffs. "Like you're going to know what's going on in the land of the giants!"

"Actually, I do know that." My stomach twirls with worry while I contemplate how much to tell them.

Hildr's hand twitches over her sword hilt again. "What do you mean?"

"That's right. I haven't had a chance to tell you." I take a deep breath and let it out in a rush. "I was kidnapped by a frost giant and taken to Jotunheim. The frost giant turned out to be Loki. He took me there because I wanted to talk to him. He said he was saving me from Mistress Sigrun's punishment and that he was going to answer the questions that I was so urgent to ask him. That's where I ran into the army he is building."

"Loki's building an army?" Britta asks.

"Yes, Loki is building an army. As I told the dragons, I don't know what to do with this information. He says he is building it for Asgard. I don't believe that it's to fight against Asgard, but we must remain alert."

"That deceiving scum!" Hildr exclaims.

"I mostly agree with you, Hildr. But remember, he did mark me with magic and then the three of you with magic. That magic will probably come to use and help protect Asgard. This is where it gets confusing. He has been helping the dragons the whole time with the dragon alliance agreement and representing them to Odin, but at the same time, he's been stealing their eggs as a zmey. He is caring for the eggs and baby dragons, but they are also being trained to carry dwarf giants and fight."

Britta scratches her head. "What a strange army."

"Yes, it is." I rub my arm, deep in thought over what has happened in the recent past. "I should go and tell the mistress I'm back, I guess."

"What for?" Hildr asks. "She sent you away, probably hoping for your death."

"We don't know that for sure. Perhaps the mistress had other intentions and was only worried about the souls for Valhalla. At least I could help in that way, seeing as I can't reap souls." I gaze at Eir, and she nods.

"It's always good to keep an open mind. You never know what other people are thinking. Others may often have good intentions but play them out in the wrong way."

"Oh." Hildr scoffs. "You always take that position, Eir, and it's rather annoying."

Eir shrugs, undeterred. "We do know that Mistress Sigrun's heart is set on protecting Asgard and Odin. She is loyal to a T in that respect. So we should give her the benefit of the doubt. From what Britta said about Rota, we also know that the winged Valkyries can be stripped, dewinged, and classed as a traitor to the Valkyries if she sides with us. That is quite a harsh punishment."

We walk inside the academy. As I pass the dining room, a waft of delicious food comes our way, assaulting our noses.

Hildr groans. "I'm starved. I need to eat."

"I'm going to continue forward. I think I shouldn't put off seeing the mistress. I've already been a long time, as Elan hijacked me and took me to the wastelands to tell them the news. I've already lost more than half a day. I don't think the mistress is going to be impressed if I leave it any longer."

"If she even expects you back," Hildr says, not bothering to hide her sarcasm. "I still think she sent you to your death."

"I guess I'll soon find out."

We part ways, and I find my way to the mistress's office. A gruff voice answers my knock. "It's open."

I'm greeted by the statues that almost look like shrines to the winged Valkyries. Their presence in her room is overpowering. Even though the academy is for both winged and wingless Valkyries, not a single statue of a wingless Valkyrie is displayed in her office, showing off her biased opinion of the wingless Valkyries. She peers up from paperwork, her eyes condescending and full of disapproval. "Oh. You're back."

- CHAPTER FOUR -

While entering the office, I look into the mistress's hardened eyes, and Hildr's thoughts run through my mind. "We're you not expecting me back, Mistress?"

"I wasn't sure what they would do with you." Her voice is harsh and offensive. "But I didn't care. Several souls for Valhalla are much more important than a mere wingless Valkyrie.

That's several souls that we wouldn't have to fight for."

"And for that, I'm happy to be of help. That is my way of contributing to Valhalla, even though I didn't have a choice. I did go in peace once I realized what the exchange was."

Her eyes narrow. "How do you take this as your contribution? I was the one who bargained the price."

"Yet it was I who went peacefully in the end. In fact, after all this time believing that the angels of death are enemies, I was surprised to find out how well they treated me."

Mistress Sigrun huffs, looking displeased. "Just my luck! So did you at least find out where they're based?"

"No. They blindfolded me the whole way there and on the way back. There's no way for me to tell where they are based. And if I did find out, they said they would uproot and move locations. Apparently, this is normal practice every time they think their position is compromised."

The mistress sits in silence, her face seething as she twirls her pen.

"So is there anything in particular you need me to do next, Mistress?"

"You could at least tell me what she wanted you for." She holds up a hand. "Wait! Let me change that. I don't care why she wanted you as long as she isn't asking you to betray Asgard."

"Do you really think she's betraying Asgard when she is giving over several souls to Asgard's cause in exchange for chatting with me?"

"No. I guess you're right. You may attend classes as per usual. It's lunchtime at the moment. I gather you're hungry." She flicks her hand and grumbles, "You're dismissed."

"Thank you, Mistress," I say with sincerity as I walk out the door.

She actually considered that I might be hungry. Even though her words and mannerisms were harsh, it was the kindest gesture she has given me in a long time, other than the time she saved my life purely so that we could win the war against the dark elves.

With a growling stomach, I make my way to the dining hall and grab a plate then load it with blueberry pancakes and fresh fruit before drizzling maple syrup over the top. It's not my regular lunchtime meal, but I missed out on breakfast.

I spot Hildr, Eir, and Britta at the table and make my way over to them. I sit down next to Britta.

Most of Asgard is not fertile with plants, and I often wondered where they received all the produce from. But after visiting Midgard and seeing other realms, I realize that they must be harvesting it from the other realms. As I slip a morsel of the blueberry pancake into my mouth, I am very thankful for that. They are delicious.

Hildr watches me, her eyes full of curiosity. She stares at me as I cut another morsel of pancake, slide it into my mouth, and chew it slowly, savoring the flavor.

"Well?" Hildr stares at me from under an arched auburn eyebrow, her impatience shining through in its usual colors.

I chew a few more times and swallow. "I guess you could say that the mistress was surprisingly lenient, which is a nice change." I cut off another piece of pancake and devour it, almost groaning in pleasure at the flavor. I didn't realize I was so hungry until I started eating. It reminds me that I hadn't had anything to eat since lunch yesterday.

Hildr scoffs. "Mistress Sigrun was nice to a wingless Valkyrie? I doubt it!"

I swallow. "Well, she didn't punish me because I was late and didn't scrutinize me by saying I didn't have any helpful information."

"Yeah, because she's punished you enough already," Hildr says condescendingly.

I'm nudged harshly from behind, and I swing forward toward the table. I look up to see Prima walking past and Mist following, twirling her long golden locks while she stares at us. They file past, one by one, with Rota following behind. Rota's eyes are full of angst, even though a hard expression occupies her face. She no longer leads her group of Valkyries. Now Prima seems to be the one who is calling the shots, especially when it comes to how they treat wingless Valkyries.

Prima and Mist plunk themselves down at the table, and something falls into my lap as Rota passes. I glance down to see a folded piece of parchment resting on my lap. Discreetly, I pick it up and unfold it under the protection of the table.

It reads, "I hope you're okay. I didn't want any part of handing you over to the angels of death, so I left. I don't know what Mistress was thinking by sending you away and possibly getting you mugged. I'm just glad you're back and in one piece. Please forgive me for not showing my friendship and appreciation of you in public, but I can't afford the defamation, as this will also affect my family. If this happens, we may lose our wings. I hope you understand this is not anything against you. Despite what you think, I do support you."

I refold the parchment and tuck it into my pocket. I'll have to destroy it later so that it doesn't get pointed back to Rota. Despite the harshness of it, I understand where she's coming from.

"Would you look at that traitor?"

I turn to find Hildr squinting at Rota. I shake my head, and my fingers play with the edges of the parchment in my pocket. "I don't think she is, Hildr. I think she has a lot to lose and can't afford to lose it. She can't associate publicly with the wingless Valkyries. Give them time. It may all change."

Hildr huffs. "I doubt it."

"She does have a lot to lose, Hildr," Britta says. "I've seen it from her sisters."

"I don't care. They should be open and honest about it."

"And what would you do if they were dewinged and unable to go to Midgard and reap souls? Asgard needs all the help it can get."

"Then they should give us the gift. We can help."

"I know, but that is never going to happen."

- CHAPTER FIVE -

Mistress Sigrun taps the chalkboard with her long stick, pointing at individual dots. It is almost impossible to see the indicated images because all the winged Valkyries are seated in front of us, blocking our view. Mistress Sigrun's favorites always sit at the front, leaving the wingless Valkyries at the back of her classroom.

The mistress studies the room, skimming over every Valkyrie. "It has come to my attention that some of you find the angels of death handsome." She lets out a disgusted sound and shakes her head. "I don't know how this is possible, but you need to pull your heads straight. Valkyries and angels of death do not mix. They are the enemies of our race, not potential mates. You are better off associating with the warriors that you've reaped. I, for one, can't understand how you can see past the horrible stench of the angels of death. Not only that, these are vicious, malicious beings."

I clear my throat, and the mistress's eyes land on me. "Being one that has visited the angels of death, I would have to disagree. Yes, they do stink. They aren't malicious, though. They are following their goals and what they are required to do—just like us. If we concentrated on the strong warriors rather than the kind, more forgiving warriors, we wouldn't have any problem with them. We wouldn't have to fight them."

The mistress looks down her nose at me. "Young wingless, even though you may have been around, you don't know them. You haven't been in a position where you have to fight them constantly. You are one of the ones that I am concerned about. You have your eyes on certain members and associate with them. You disgust me how you are willing to associate with and befriend the enemy."

"Is that so? Then why did you sacrifice me to them? Instead of being harmed, I was just taken to meet Freya. Although they were suspicious of me, they didn't mistreat me, and I came back in one piece, as you can see." I wave a hand up and down my body, pointing out the obvious.

Mist sits in the corner, twirling her blond locks. "Ah, Mistress Sigrun, we don't want to share our boys with her. Besides, she's just a wingless Valkyrie. Who cares who she associates with?"

The winged Valkyries nod in agreement, and Prima's face wears a condescending expression. I look at Rota, but she casts her eyes to the ground.

The mistress looks toward Mist. "You're right. We don't care what the wingless Valkyries think of them. They aren't genuine stock for our reproduction anyway. As for the wingless, they could disappear from Asgard for weeks, and we wouldn't miss them."

Kara! Elan's voice projects through my head. *Kara! I hope you can hear me. You need to bring all your fighters out here now. There's trouble brewing around Odin's castle.*

"Are you sure?" I ask out loud.

Mistress Sigrun gives me a weird look. "Of course I'm sure. We don't need you. Since when do we need you?"

I frown at her in confusion then suddenly remember the conversation she was having with me.

Elan's voice enters my head again. *Yes, I'm sure! We need you and anyone you can find. Grab them and bring them here now.*

"Where are the senior Valkyries?" I ask Mistress Sigrun.

The mistress lifts her chin and stares down her nose at me. "None of your business."

Elan's voice continues to speak in my head. *I don't know. So far, I haven't found them. I don't think they know what is happening.*

I look at Mistress Sigrun, taking in her defiant features. She appears as though she is holding information from me on purpose. "I'm talking to Elan."

The mistress huffs, but before she can express her disapproval, I continue.

"We need to leave now. The palace is under attack."

The color drains out of Mistress Sigrun's face. "Are you sure?"

I nod. "Yes. Elan wouldn't make up a stupid story like that. It would have to be true."

"Winged Valkyries, let's go." The mistress's battle side kicks in, and she commands the academy fighters.

Hildr stands as though ready to fight, and her fingers twitch over her sword hilt. "What about the wingless Valkyries?"

The mistress looks over her nose at Hildr. "You don't have the fighting skills the others do."

Hildr raises her chin, imitating the mistress. "The difference is much slimmer these days. And besides, we have dragons."

Mistress Sigrun rolls her eyes at us. "You think dragons are the answer to everything."

Eir stands next to Hildr. "No. But they certainly help us fight, and you've seen it. You're just too stubborn to admit that we're right and that you need our help."

"I am not stubborn. I am making judgments on what I know is right."

Britta stands next to Eir. "We want to help protect Asgard, too, Mistress. And any fighting skills would be better than none."

The mistress looks thoughtful for a moment before she nods. "Okay. Do whatever you want. I don't expect much from you, but if you insist on coming, then come."

"Oh, I feel the love," Hildr says sarcastically.

All of the Valkyries exit the room, grabbing their weapons from the hold on the way out. I grab my favorite quiver and arrows and slide my sword between the quiver and my back. I loop my sling onto my back pocket. Elan didn't say what was attacking the palace, so we don't know what we are up against exactly. Hildr, Eir, Britta, and I run down the hall and out the front door of the academy.

"Elan!" I call. "Elllaaan!"

It's only a matter of moments before she suddenly appears not far from the academy and lands. A few of the winged Valkyries clutch their chests. They haven't gotten used to her appearing out of nowhere, changing from invisible to visible.

I chuckle briefly. These are supposed to be seasoned warriors, yet they flinch when a friendly dragon suddenly appears.

I run up to Elan, and I'm about to ask her to call the other dragons when I hear three different thumps land beside me on all sides. I spin to see that Drogon, Naga, and Tanda have landed, ready to help us. "You're one step ahead of me." I laugh, looking at Elan. "Good thinking."

The four dragons slip down to their haunches, and each rider climbs on to her dragon's back. The saddles are already mounted and ready to go. Drogon, Tanda, and Naga push into the air, and Elan turns invisible, following them not long afterward. I pull my dragon-scale coat out of the pouch and slide it on.

The dragons fly toward the castle, and it takes only a few minutes before I can see it in the distance. I look down at open fields filled by dark elves outside the palace walls. Elan was not exaggerating. I pull at my cloak and wrap it around me, covering every part of my body so I am invisible with her.

She throws her head back and bellows out a roar. The faces of the dark elves look toward the sky. They would be unable to see Elan approaching. She swings down and flicks them aside. She keeps doing this until, eventually, I spot the dark elves who invaded Asgard last time and fought the Valkyries. I zero in on the one that had threatened my friends and me.

The chief elf stares up in our direction. He wouldn't be able to see anything but the sky above him. His hands do something strange, and I expect to feel a wave of magic coming my way, but nothing happens.

Elan flies lower, ready to grasp him within her teeth. But when she gets close, she collides with something invisible. She flips, twists, and struggles to fly straight for a moment, tossing me from side to side as she battles to steady herself.

"What was that, Elan?"

I'm not sure. But maybe he has a protective barrier around him, because I couldn't grasp him between my teeth.

I spin and gaze down at the chief dark elf in time to spot a strange satisfied expression plastered across his face. Even though Elan is invisible, he must've known that she hit his barrier.

"I told you not to intervene, young wingless." His voice chills me to the bone as he yells up at me. "I told you if you did that, I would rip the limbs off your friends, one by one, yet you're still getting involved. You mustn't care much for your friends."

The chief dark elf flicks his hands to the side, and I assume that he is aiming at something until I notice that he has positioned his fingers into claws. I follow the direction of his hand, losing all feeling in my face. Eir is flung off Naga's back, her body pitching to the side. There is nothing that can soften the fall.

Naga's eyes widen, and he abruptly spins around, trying to catch up with Eir. He flaps his wings furiously, beating against the wind, desperate to catch her. He paddles his feet, trying to create more speed. Amazingly, he gains traction. I open my mouth to yell encouragement when suddenly Eir vanishes. My jaw drops, and my eyes dart frantically around, searching for her. My heart sinks. I can't find her anywhere.

- CHAPTER SIX -

Naga flies to the spot we last saw Eir, frantically hunting the area where she disappeared. A distinct look of hopelessness passes over his face, intensifying with each moment.

"No!" I rip the hood off my head, pull the bow off my back, and nock an arrow, drawing it to my line of sight. I maneuver it around until the chief dark elf is my target. He faces the opposite direction, focusing on Odin's castle. "Elan, steady." The bow is taut, and I long to let it fly, but I want the aim to be true.

Elan flaps her wings, keeping her body as still as possible as I release the arrow. It flies directly at the dark elf. It's almost silent as it flies through the air, directly at him. The aim is true to his heart. At the last second, the chief elf holds up his hand in a stopping motion, and the arrow halts before clattering to the ground.

He spins around slowly and looks into the air, spotting my head in the distance. I didn't even have time to re-cover my head with my dragon-scale cloak to make me invisible again. "There you are, wingless. I warned you. You cannot blame me for what I have warned you about. The disappearance of your friend rests solely on you."

Before I can answer, a loud cry streams past me in a brown blur, heading straight for the chief dark elf. Hildr lets out the war cry as Drogon plummets headfirst to the ground, the chief dark elf in his sight. Hildr is several hundred feet away, and the dark elf spins and waves his hands, thrusting them in her direction. I gasp as she is jolted out of Drogon's saddle and flung backward through the air. She shoots back a fair distance then drops dramatically toward the ground.

Drogon bellows a roar and labors to spin around and fly in the opposite direction. Even with all his expertise in flying, he can't maneuver quickly enough to catch her before she falls.

A red streak flashes through the air, aiming for Hildr. Britta rides on Tanda's back, and they nose-dive toward Hildr. Their plummeting rate has me clenching my teeth, yet Tanda tucks her wings tighter to her side, increasing her speed to reach Hildr.

But Hildr remains out of their reach. Panic explodes off her face.

"Try your magic," I yell while pulling on mine at the same time. It's not gathering quickly enough. I'm not sure it will work anyway, but I'm grasping at straws. Everything is happening so fast.

Something blue streaks low and dives toward Hildr. It's Naga. Waves of excitement course through me. He nudges her, breaking some of her fall, yet she still tumbles at a harmful speed. She flops to the ground and cries out in pain. The cries send shivers down my spine, but at the same time, I know that is a good sign. Hildr grasps her right shoulder and rolls slowly off that side, letting out another scream of pain before holding her hip as well. She is in no position to fight. Even her Valkyrie healing powers will take too long to bring her back to fighting capacity. I'm surprised that her injuries are not worse, and I silently give thanks to Naga's quick moves.

Naga lands, waddles up to Hildr, and nudges her face lightly. His face is so distraught, reminding me that Eir is missing.

Drogon lands next to him, his face a reflection of Naga's.

Elan lands next to them, and Naga looks at the sky. *No!*

That one word turns my stomach into a tornado of worry. I glance up to see Britta charging for the dark elf. Her hands are working in a circle in front of her, and her face is determined.

Tanda isn't as fast as the other dragons, but she's still giving it a good go. Her speed is rather impressive. Britta and Tanda nose-dive toward the seemingly unaware chief dark elf. Britta thrusts her hands at the dark elf, unleashing her untrained magic. Seconds later, a bright light erupts around the dark elf in the shape of a semicircle curving over the top and down around him. He must have secured a defensive barrier around him, stopping all attacks of magic.

Slowly, the chief dark elf spins, his mouth cocked on one side in a snarl.

I want to jump on Elan's back, fly to him, and remove that smile right off his face. First, though, I need to attend to Hildr. I slide off Elan's back and land next to Hildr. She looks twisted, and her hip is caved in on one side. She is holding in her moans, yet I can see that she is in extraordinary pain. I have to move her and somehow get her onto Elan's back so that I can take her to Anita. I clench my teeth as I assess the best way to transport her without hurting her.

A shrill war cry emanates from above. When I turn, I spot Britta weaving her hands in a circle, gathering her magic as she readies to shoot at the dark elf again. Before she can unleash her magic at him, the chief elf thrusts his hands in her direction.

"Look out, Britta!" I scream.

Tanda darts to the side, narrowly missing the bolt of magic soaring in her direction, yet it manages to clip Britta on her shoulder. The force shoves her shoulder backward, and she struggles to hang on to the saddle and the straps, which are the only things keeping her on Tanda's back.

Realizing she's not hitting the elf any with magic, Britta grabs the hilt of her sword and draws it out in one fluid motion. She throws her arm forward, and the sword flings through the air, gaining distance and heading straight toward the dark elf. The sword flies at an impressive pace. Somehow, the chief dark elf manages to catch sight of the approaching sword. He knocks it out of the way before it reaches him then spins it around with his magic and sends it back in Britta's direction. Britta flinches when the sword is a few feet away, and she darts to the side as it spins overhead. She reaches up and catches it in an impressive move.

I let out a whistle. I'm impressed, although Britta carries on as though nothing spectacular happened. Her jaw is clenched with determination as she sets her gaze on the dark elf again.

I hold my breath. I should be out there, helping her. First, I have to get Hildr to Anita. I scramble to Hildr, only to be reminded that Drogon is already there. He nudges her face gently, keeping his many horns away from her. I want to slap my hand on my forehead. How did I not think of Drogon? Of course he is there by Hildr's side.

"Drogon, we need to get Hildr to Anita back at the academy. Can you take her?"

Dragon nudges Hildr again, and she gives him a half-smile. Even though the pain is evident in her eyes, she is trying to make Drogon worry less. The bond is so strong between these two.

Dragon pulls his eyes away from Hildr. *I want to look after Hildr very much, but I want to rip that dark elf's head off first. Perhaps Naga can take her.*

Naga moves forward and sniffs Hildr. His big blue eyes are filled with sadness, and he cringes slightly when Hildr groans. *Naga be happy to take Hildr to healer. One moment.*

Naga pushes off into the sky.

"Where are you going, Naga?" I call after him.

Naga must avenge Eir first.

I follow Naga's progress into the sky. If I weren't watching him the entire way, he would almost be invisible. His color blends in perfectly. He is the slightest bit darker than the sky on a clear day, but with the aid of the white dots on his wings, he blends in. Suddenly, Naga dives, and cries ring out from the middle of the field. Dark elves shoot up into the air and flip. Underneath them, a blue streak charges forward, headbutting every dark elf in the road on his way back to Hildr's side.

"Naga, way to go!" I say when he stops next to Hildr.

Naga not happy. Naga wants Eir. Naga want to punish dark elves for what they did to Eir. His voice cracks on the last sentence. *Naga needs to find out.*

"And we will definitely see what we can do as soon as we can, Naga. Eir is our friend, too, but right now, we need to get Hildr some help." I stroke his nose, and I think I see moisture gather in the corner of his eye.

Several dark elves move toward us. Drogon nudges Hildr gently then tucks his chin and charges toward the elves, horns first. *Take care of Hildr, Naga.* After he bowls them over, Drogon pushes off into the air, swoops down, clasps Hildr in his talons, and places her gently on Naga's back. Then he takes to the sky. Seconds later, he dive-bombs toward another group, releasing a large plume of fire over our attackers.

I secure Hildr on the blue dragon's back. "You might have trouble getting her inside the building."

That's okay. Naga roar loudly. If doesn't work, Naga set the building on fire.

"Oh no. Don't do that." I stare at him in shock. "Your roar should work fine. If it doesn't, you can speak to Anita in her mind. I'm sure she will come out."

Naga will work it out.

Naga pushes off into the sky. I watch them fly for a couple of minutes, pulling away when a movement on top of a mountain catches my eye. I squint, studying the spot. I think I see Gilroma, except he seems to be lurking in the shadows. I close one eye and try to focus, but I can't quite make the figure out, although several features of the person remind me of him. I climb onto Elan and pull my hood over my head. Elan takes to the sky, turning invisible. I'm about to direct her to the top of the mountain to have a closer look, when I hear a massive yell behind me.

- CHAPTER SEVEN -

I clasp harder on Elan's straps as we spin around and fly in that direction. Her body meets my request without words spoken. It is almost like our minds have merged.

A surge of fire shoots out of Tanda's mouth, aimed directly at the dark elves near her. For some reason, they are more concentrated in that area, and it worries me that Britta isn't on Tanda's back. I can't see her anywhere. I rapidly search the area, coming up empty. Tanda lands and stomps forward, pushing back more dark elves. When they clear, I spot something on the ground. It's Britta. She is sprawled out, injured, and Tanda has worked her way to stand over the top of my friend.

A couple of dark elves gather courage and progress forward. Tanda shoots a long plume of fire toward them, blocking their path with a warning. I gaze down at Britta. Her leg looks twisted in the wrong direction.

"Come, Elan. We need to intervene."

You don't need to tell me. Elan had already changed course before I finished speaking the words. She nose-dives toward the dark elves, both of us in our invisible form.

Quickly, I push back my hood, grab my bow and arrow, then pull my hood over my head again. I nock an arrow, aim it directly at one of the dark elves, and release the string.

I hold my breath and steady my heart as the arrow heads straight at the elf. I don't want to get too excited until the arrow meets its mark. The arrow continues through the air. If there is a barrier in place, the arrow pierces through it and digs into the dark elf's side. He cries out in pain. As the elf grasps hold of the arrow shaft, I cheer inwardly. The elf is distracted from any fighting and clasps the shaft sticking out of his hip.

He searches the sky, looking for the culprit. I release the next arrow and watch as it aims directly toward him. He waves his hand, knocking the arrow off its path and to the side.

I groan when his eyes fix on me. Even though Elan is invisible and my dragon-scale cloak turns invisible when touching her, my face and any other skin not under the coat's protection are still visible. I know he can see my face under the hood of my cape.

He flicks a hand at me, shooting me with magic, and I block it with my own. Even though there are many Valkyries and dark elves fighting underneath me, I feel as though I am fighting this war alone. Eir is missing, Hildr is at Anita's, and Britta should be joining her soon.

In the brief moment I have before the dark elf attacks me again, I take in the scene below me. The Valkyries line the side of Odin's palace as the elves try to push forward. The slain Valkyries and dark elves remain in the center of the war field.

Elan swerves, and a surge of magic flies past, narrowly missing us.

"Thanks, Elan."

No problem. She veers up, and the dark elf's eyes don't leave me as he sends more magic my way. I notice a line of dark elves pushing forward toward Odin's palace, breaking the line of Valkyries. I glance down to assess the situation. It doesn't look good for the Valkyries.

Drogon pushes forward and lands on the area before the palace. He shoots forth a large plume of fire at the elves that have broken through the line of Valkyries. Then the brown dragon stomps forward, scooping dark elves into his mouth and flinging them aside.

I tear my attention away. I must watch the dark elf, whose attention I've clasped, to see if I can pick up his next plan of attack. A wave of relief washes over me when I spot Tanda leaping toward him. She shoots out a bolt of fire at the dark elf. It hits the elf directly, and he cries out in pain as his sleeve catches on fire. He must've been focusing on me, because Tanda's attack surprised him.

Hastily, the dark elf slaps his arm, trying to smother the fire. As soon as he extinguishes it, he twirls his hand and gathers magic to use against Tanda. Quickly, I load another arrow and release it his way, pushing it faster with my magic. It hits him in the hip right after he releases his magic at Tanda.

"Tanda, look out!" I cry, feeling great relief when she maneuvers out of the way before my warning.

Her red eyes focus on me, filled with respect, and she nods my way as an indication of thanks.

"We've got you covered." I motion to Britta. "Take Britta to Anita, our healer. She can't fight like that, and you'll be less distracted if Britta is not underneath you."

Tanda gazes down at Britta, her face contorting as she hears her rider's moans of pain.

"She can't walk, Tanda. Her legs are broken. I can see it from here. Can you carry her gently in your teeth?"

Tanda's eyes fill with worry, and her expression is pained. *Are you serious?* Panic laces her voice. *I'll hurt her, even if I am gentle.*

"No matter who moves her, it is going to hurt her. I have faith in you, Tanda. I know you care for her. I'm sure you can be gentle if you want to, even inside your teeth."

Tanda gently scoops her teeth around my friend, flinching when Britta groans again in pain.

"It's okay, Tanda," I call down to her, seeing her worried look. "Britta can't stay in the middle of a battlefield like that. It's too hard to protect her, and she can't defend herself. There's a greater chance of her being killed. She won't even have enough strength to conjure her magic. She needs to be moved."

Dark elves start to close in around her, and I shoot a bolt of magic at them before unleashing a couple of arrows at a dark elf distracted by Tanda. Instantly, the dark elf's attention is pulled away from Tanda and my injured friend, and he retaliates by shooting magic my way.

Rapidly, Elan drops then dodges another bolt of magic coming from another dark elf. With my heart thumping rapidly in my chest, I am grateful for her quick reactions. So much is going on that I can't always pick the biggest threat. Elan spins sideways, and I secure my hood over my head completely, causing us to disappear from the dark elf's sight.

I take this opportunity to have a good look around and assess the situation. Senior Valkyries and dark elves lie motionless in the middle of the field. I just hope that the Valkyries aren't dead and only unconscious. My mind struggles over what it has seen and dealt with already in the battle, and my emotions rise to the surface, reminding me that I thought I spotted Gilroma on the mountaintop before. Surely if he is around, he would help my side like he has helped me master parts of my magic. It would be beneficial because he is a dark elf, aware of their ways and familiar with their magic.

A movement catches my eye, and I focus on the spot in the distance. I see a bald man, and I call to Elan. "I think I see Gilroma on that mountain over there. But if it is him, I can't understand why he is hovering in the background."

Which mountain? Her head moves as though she is studying different mountainsides.

"The one straight ahead but just off to the right. About one o'clock."

She turns to the mountain and concentrates on that spot. *It is him, I think. It looks like him in the distance anyway.*

"Let's go see what he's doing up there. Maybe he's the one that made Eir disappear." Deep down, I know I am allowing myself to get caught up in false hopes, but I also know that I need some hope to help me go on, or else I will be blown away by grief. "Maybe she's fine, and she's just disappeared. Maybe he's going to look after her and keep her safe until she recovers."

Elan flies in the direction of the mountain, and my heart rises with each flap of her wings. Gilroma has been a patient mentor and has often made me feel better about things that have happened. I gaze down at the battle below us. It still looks nasty. Maybe Gilroma knows something that will help us.

When I stare back at the location where I spotted him, he has disappeared. I search the rest of the mountaintop. "Where did he go?"

Elan flies in silence. *I can't spot him anywhere. Maybe he has disappeared behind a boulder. I only glanced away for a second.*

"Me too." I fiddle with the saddle straps, twisting them in annoyance. "Gilroma!" I call. When he doesn't answer, I call again. "Gilroma!"

Elan lands on the mountaintop. The terrain is made of harsh stone. I climb off Elan's back and search the area behind the boulders. "Why would he disappear from me?" I mutter, half to myself and half to Elan. "Surely he must've seen me flying in his direction."

Elan shrugs.

I search around a few more boulders. "Elan, can you please sniff him out? I can't see him anywhere."

Her nostrils labor as she sniffs the air, trying to capture the scent. She screws up her nose. *Are you sure you can trust him?*

"He hasn't given me any reason not to, Elan. He's taught me some magic, and he has healed my wounds. He even knew that I was marked by magic. He helped me work with it and express it better. He knows I am bent on protecting Asgard. Why would he help me with all these things if he didn't have Asgard's safety in mind?"

She shrugs and moves forward. *I don't know. I just have a funny feeling in the pit of my stomach.*

"I don't. But it is strange if he's up here and not helping us. He would be able to see the fight happening below us, and he could have helped Eir. He could have helped heal Hildr and Britta's injuries also."

My point exactly. He's not acting like someone with your best interest at heart. She sniffs some more and continues working around the mountain. *Although it's strange, I definitely saw him, and it smells like him, but I can't see him anywhere.* She frowns, and her scales clump on her forehead.

"Perhaps he is going to get help," I say.

Elan's frown deepens. *I doubt it. And no, he's definitely not here. He's gone.*

- CHAPTER EIGHT -

Disheartened, I climb onto Elan's back. A headache grows from all the scenarios going through my mind.

"I don't get it, Elan. Why would he hang around watching the Valkyries struggle against the dark elves yet not help?" I peer over the edge. "I'm sure he could see that they are at a disadvantage because they don't have magic, and the dark elves are using theirs freely." We sit motionless for a moment. "Even with all the fighting experience that the Valkyries have, it has minimal success against confident magic-wielding beings."

I am saddened as I gaze across the battlefield. I have magic, but I am only one person. "Where is Thor and his wonderous hammer, Mjolnir? And where are Loki and the dragon army he said he is raising to protect Asgard?" I sigh, swimming in hopelessness. "I'm stuck here with only four dragons, wondering what to do. That's nothing compared to an army of over sixty dwarf-giant riders. We could really use Loki's army's help."

Yeah, where is he? Elan's voice explodes with annoyance. *He steals the dragons then doesn't turn up to work with us as he promised. Don't get me started.* She stomps her foot, and several rocks scatter from under her.

I'm deep in thought when, through the haze, I remember the little winged trinket that

Freya gave me. I pull off my dragon-scale cloak and slide my quiver off my back. The silver charm with a horn lying across a set of wings dangles from a loop on my quiver. Holding it in my fingers, I rub my thumb across the hard surface like I did the day Freya gave it to me. I don't think this is what Freya meant when she said to tell her any information I found out, but since Loki isn't here to help defend Asgard, I should call her. She seemed genuine, like she wanted to help us. Maybe she will.

I am lost in thought as I rub my thumb continuously over the silver wings. Despite the angels of death being our fighting enemies, Freya seemed lovely and not like someone who would want to see Asgard come to harm, even though the angels of death and the Valkyries are constantly battling over the souls. Unintentionally, I continue to rub my thumb over the wings, too lost in thought to realize what I am doing.

I'm startled when a voice that is not Elan's or any of the dragons' enters my head. It is lined with sweetness and tinted with a soft seduction.

Kara. You have called so soon. Have you found out some news about the new army?

"Freya. I'm so sorry. I didn't mean to bother you. I was thinking about you while deep in thought and absentmindedly stroked the wings." In case she got angry, I thought the half-truth would go better.

I can hear the smile in Freya's voice. *That's okay. What are you thinking about? Perhaps I can help.*

"That is what I was wondering and hoping when I was absentmindedly rubbing the wings." I release the wings in a motion that suggests it was an accident. "Asgard is under attack by the dark elves. It's not looking good. And I don't know where Thor and Loki are." I set my voice to almost pleading. "We need your help. If we don't defeat them, then Odin and his palace are going to be attacked. The dark elves attacked us not long ago, and they told me then that their mission is to kill Odin and take over the castle and Asgard. As you know, this will not be good for the angels of death and peace amongst the realms."

I understand. Just give us a few moments. Keep the battle up. Don't give up.

She breaks the connection. I'm not sure exactly what she has in mind, but a slight feeling of relief sinks in.

A blue flash catches my eye, distracting me from my thoughts. Naga has tucked his wings tightly by his side and is nose-diving toward a group of dark elves. At the last second, he unfurls his wings to flatten out his descent and angles horizontally over the ground, headbutting several of the dark elves off their feet. Several Valkyries spot him just in time and dart away, either with their wings or by moving to the side. The dark elves are knocked away like bowling pins, and I can't help but smile at the sight. They look ridiculous. When Naga's diving momentum slows to a stop, he lifts his head and shakes it with his tongue hanging out the side.

I chuckle. "Naga looks like a goof."

As quickly as he descended, Naga pushes off the ground and returns to the sky. Suddenly, something large shoots at Naga and hits him in the side. He veers sideways, flopping awkwardly.

"Naga!" I scream, feeling hopeless as he careens, back first, toward the ground.

Drogon streaks past. He dives and dodges, managing to get under Naga's unconscious body just before he hits the ground. Drogon's body caves slightly upon the impact, although he manages to take some of the weight and soften Naga's fall.

He struggles with a balancing act as he pushes up, laboring under the additional weight of the smaller dragon. My heart sinks as I watch them disappear from the battlefield. I cross my fingers, hoping that Naga will be all right.

I search for the item that hit him, but there is nothing that big lying around. It must have been magic, but I'm not sure. It happened so quickly.

More weight piles onto my shoulders. I'm the only uninjured wingless Valkyrie with magic. I long to see if Naga is okay, but I know I must stay and help the Valkyries fight. I'm sure Drogon will look after him. Asgard depends on me, and so do the Valkyries.

In front of the palace, a line of winged Valkyries fights notoriously against the dark elves. Mistress Sigrun is one of the many in the line. They are holding the line well, but I can see their fatigue from here. A dark elf blocks many Valkyrie attacks with magic then shoots back with several bolts of magic in a row. These bolts hit a senior Valkyrie directly in her chest and head, and she collapses to the ground, unmoving. The dark elf knocks her aside and stomps over her, followed by a few more elves. They break through the Valkyries' barrier to the palace.

The faces of the soldiers on the ramparts are plastered with terror as they gather their courage to take on these unfairly advantaged magic beings. They are the last line of defense for Asgard before Odin's palace falls. Another dark elf manages to break his way through the barrier and charge toward the castle.

Elan dives toward the progressing dark elves, without waiting for my instruction, and scorches them with her fire before they can move any farther. Because she is invisible, her attack would have come out of nowhere, finishing the dark elves before they knew what was happening.

The dark elves throw themselves on their backs and roll around, trying to extinguish the fire. If only the dragons could do that with all of the dark elves, but it would be too risky. The dark elves on the battlefield are too close to the Valkyries.

I search for the chief dark elf, the one that threatened to harm my friends and who has carried out much of his promise. He is still fighting within the front lines, with his hand holding the large gash in his side. He must be in so much pain, but I don't feel pity for him. Swords are clanging in battle, each strike blocked as the welder maneuvers. The sounds of swords sliding against swords ring out, creating a different kind of music. It grinds in my ears, filling me with disdain for battle. But the fight is far from over.

Elan lands on the palace side of the battle. I climb off my invisible dragon's back, and my cloak turns into golden scales as soon as my connection with Elan is broken. Everyone around me is too preoccupied to notice my arrival.

I wish I could gather enough magic to stop the fighting altogether, but I can't. Still, I need to do something to help prevent this. I gather a large amount of magic together, hoping it will be enough, then fling it between the Valkyries in the front row and the elves that are fighting them. Hopefully, I have created a safety barrier. It seems to work, but I need a lot more to protect all the Valkyries, or else this effort will also be useless. I strain, trying to stretch the magic further, trying to weave it around and in between every Valkyrie and dark elf in the front row not far from me.

As I push out the magic, I can feel my energy draining from my body. The barrier takes a lot of effort and concentration, and I'm burning out quickly.

Looking for hope, I search the fields and mountaintop again but come up empty. I can't find Gilroma anywhere. I don't understand where he would have gone that was more important than helping us. I know he's afraid to come out and be seen because he's a dark elf, but he's not the same as them. He is much shorter and stockier with glowing yellow eyes. The others are tall and lean with long hair and dark, evil eyes. Surely that would be enough to distinguish him from the others.

My arms are starting to lose feeling as the weakness from the drained energy sinks in. I push my magic barrier forward, trying my best to ignore the fact that I could collapse at any moment. I don't know what else to do.

I try to push the barrier out farther, but I just can't. Out of nowhere, dark elves rise into the air then are flung off to the side. Elan has remained in her invisible form and is picking them off one at a time. A giggle rises to my throat, climbing past my exhaustion, as I observe the dark elves' faces. I can only imagine what is going through their heads. The lightheartedness slightly heightens my energy supply, and I push out some more with my magic, only to find the blood draining from my face because of the exertion. My knees start to give, and I struggle to keep them straight and firmly planted on the ground. Even after pulling from all my willpower, they crumple underneath me, and I find myself falling to the ground.

- CHAPTER NINE -

A cold hand with a warm touch strokes my face. "Kara? Kara, are you all right?"

Rich, warm tones fill the voice, and I welcome it. It is like soft music accompanying a dream I don't want to leave. I must've fallen asleep and had a nightmare that changed into a blissful dream. The cold hand strokes my face again, shooting warm sensations down my spine.

"Kara. Kara, wake up. I'm worried about you."

I breathe in deeply, reveling in the warm sensation, until I realize what I am smelling. Halfway through the breath, I cough and splutter. The air reeks of corpses. My stomach lurches convulsively until, eventually, the jerking wakes me. I pry my eyes open and stare into the dreamy dark eyes of Harut.

Relief washes over his face. "Thank Freyja!" he exclaims, using one of Freya's many pronunciations of her name. "You're okay, and you've come back to me."

"Harut? What are you doing here? Am I still in Asgard?" I prop myself up on my elbows and search the area. My ears are assaulted with the ringing of swords and yelling of the wounded.

Harut chuckles, pulling my attention away from the horror. "Of course you're still in Asgard. Where else would you be?"

I push myself completely upright, resting on my arms. "I never know these days. I seem to end up in all sorts of places, often against my will." I give him a sly smile. "And besides, how did you guys even get into Asgard?"

"I'm sure you've worked out by now that Heimdall is not the only access point to Asgard, especially if you're part of one of the nine realms." He smiles, and I feel my cheeks warm.

Instantly, I chastise myself. "Do you mean Yggdrasil?"

"Of course I mean the world tree. How else do you think we can fly between the realms?"

"I wouldn't know. I don't have wings." I look around and notice that I'm not in the middle of the battle. Someone must've dragged me to the side and rested me against a boulder.

A woman's voice filled with warmth speaks from around the corner. "Kara! You're awake." Shortly afterward, Freya walks into my vision. "It looks like we got here just in time."

"Thank you, Freya. We could use your help." I frown when I spot angels of death fighting side by side with the Valkyries. "But why would you help protect Asgard?" I point at the enemies fighting together. "I never thought I would see the Valkyries and the angels of death fighting together."

"It is no good letting Asgard fall, is it?"

"Why would you care?"

"If Asgard falls, then there will be more disarray among the realms. Despite Odin being a pigheaded god, he does manage to keep the peace amongst the realms more than what other worlds would, especially ones who would want to start a war against Asgard. So it doesn't make sense for us to let Asgard fall." She studies the line of defense and frowns. A dark elf has managed to break into the barrier. Freya squats down and picks up a rock then throws it at him. The sight is extremely out of place and an uncharacteristic action for such a dainty figure. The stone hits the dark elf in the face, and he stops to rub his head, looking confused. Seeing his reaction, she huffs a laugh. "I don't understand one thing,"

"What is that?" I ask.

"Where are all your soldiers that your Valkyries reap? They are supposed to protect Asgard. Yet all I see is Valkyries fighting without their help. Isn't that the whole reason why you reap the souls? Don't the Valkyries keep them here and train them to be fantastic warriors?" She runs her hands over her long, flowing dress. "I'm sure they're not trained to be lovers like I would prefer."

"But Einherjar are supposed to be saved for Ragnarök," I say.

"Isn't this similar to what Ragnarök would be like? Or perhaps it is Ragnarök. If we don't nip this in the bud, it may blow out of proportion and turn into Ragnarök."

It was a simple explanation that slapped the realization across my face and pierced my brain with some common sense. "You're right.

Why aren't they here? I would have thought one of the senior Valkyries would have brought them out. As you said, it has similarities to how Ragnarök is predicted."

"Then why don't you hurry off and get them, child?" She shoos a hand at me.

I glance at her briefly, rebutting the immediate thought that I am not a child. But then I consider that despite her beauty, she is an ancient goddess, so to her, I would be a child.

An intense burst of heat comes from the direction of the battle, and I glance over to see a massive plume of fire shooting out of thin air. I smile to myself. An invisible Elan is behind that attack on the elves. Cries of pain reach my ear, and a sick feeling fills my stomach.

I don't like hearing that cry, no matter who it is coming from. I scramble to my feet, holding my head when a bout of dizziness takes over. Then I jog toward the hall of Valhalla. It suddenly irks me to think that the warriors have been feasting while we've been battling. Their whole lives on Valhalla have been about feasting on loads of mead between the practice battles. It's time they pay us back for some of this extravagant treatment. Hopefully, they will not be too drunk to come and fight.

I sprint to the hall doors and fling them wide before charging into the hall. Laughter and merriment of the soldiers assault my ears. It takes all of my effort to push down my anger and relax my throat. I breathe deeply from my diaphragm and project my voice from the pit of my stomach.

"Warriors! It is time to serve your realm." The room remains filled with loud chatter and laughter. So I deepen my voice. Relaxing my throat some more, I project my voice from the very bottom of my diaphragm, making sure it is loud enough to cross the room over the boisterousness of the soldiers. "Warriors! It is time for you to defend Asgard."

Silence falls over the hall, and several curious eyes land on me, filling the room with awkwardness.

Eventually, the silence is broken by a single voice. "And who might you be? You don't even have wings. Aren't we supposed to take our commands only from Odin and the beautiful battle maidens?" He turns to face the other warriors, looking for encouragement. "What do they call themselves?"

"Valkyries," one of the warriors at the far end calls.

"Ha! Yes. That's right. Valkyries."

Anger burns in my stomach, and I struggle to push it aside. "I'm a Valkyrie."

"But you don't have wings," the ringleader calls. "And you're not one of those blond beauties. So how are we supposed to believe you?"

"Have I not served you enough over time? Have you not seen Valkyries without wings serving you during your feast or cleaning your halls after you've made your mess after too much mead?"

"I've seen young lasses that have a pretty face. Some of them didn't have wings, so that would mean that they aren't Valkyries," another soldier calls from across the room.

I clench my teeth a couple of times and remind myself that these warriors are brainwashed toward the wingless Valkyries just like the rest of Asgard. Still, my eyes narrow at the soldier. "Those lasses without wings are Valkyries—just like I am." I clench my fist behind my back. I don't need to stir up a whole hall full of warriors. I don't want to be in a fight against them too.

After a moment's silence, a voice from another room calls, "I remember you." A broad-shouldered figure pushes forward, elbowing his way to the front of the crowd. He has a mead tankard still in his hand and takes another swig while moving closer, bumping the other warriors with his elbow on the way through. He stops at the front of the pack and takes another big swig of mead. It sloshes down the side of his beard. He wipes it away with his arm, his eyes never leaving me, and belches loudly. "You're that young lady that left me in pain because you couldn't reap my soul."

Instantly, my memory flashes back to the first time I was in Midgard when Harut allowed me to reap this man's soul. I felt bad that I had left him in pain, but I didn't know any better. Now as I study him, I know that this was the right side for him to come. Valkyries like the tough warriors who lack empathy. Freya wouldn't appreciate his cold-heartedness.

I raise my chin. "Yes, that was me. I did try to reap your soul and prove myself to the winged Valkyries. Unfortunately, it turns out the wingless Valkyries haven't received that gift. Odin is biased and does not pass it down to us. But that does not make me any less a Valkyrie."

"You say Odin is biased against you," the first warrior yells. "That proves that we shouldn't be taking orders from you because Odin wouldn't place that responsibility into the hands of someone he is biased against."

Anger burns deep within the pit of my stomach. I take in a sharp breath and straighten my back. "We need your assistance. Winged and wingless Valkyries are out on the battlefield right now, trying to protect Odin's palace and Asgard."

The soldier that I couldn't reap bursts out laughing. When finished, he says, "Why don't you make us? You have no powers. You can't even reap our souls and leave us in pain."

Anger burns in my body, and my magic has already gathered, lingering in the palm of my hand. The warrior's disrespect disturbs me so much that I fling my hand at him in frustration. A bolt of magic flies directly at him and strikes his foot. He jumps on the spot, grabbing his foot and whimpering.

"So I don't have powers, hey? Would anybody else like to accuse me of the same? I'm inviting you to step forward, or you could join me and come out to help us fight. If you don't, we may not have an Asgard to live in."

- CHAPTER TEN -

Within a few minutes, the hall empties, and
the einherjar grab their weapons and march to
the battlefield to take their place in defending
Asgard. As the rowdy lot follow me, I hope I
am not leading them all to slaughter. Many
years of gathering souls and training have gone
into this group. The last thing we need is to
have them slaughtered by magic. After easily
attacking the broad warrior with my magic, I

have lost much of my confidence in bringing them out. Still, the other Valkyries don't have magic, so the more warriors, the better.

As we near the battle, cries and the clanging of weapons ring out. The warriors file past me in a jog, rushing to aid the angels of death and Valkyries.

Something blue at ground level catches my eye.

"Naga?"

Naga is cowering in a crevice in the mountain. His shoulders are slumped, and he looks sad and dejected. A large stream of red blood flows down his side.

"Oh, Naga!" I charge to him. His wings hang limply by his side, and his face and eyes are filled with moisture. "Naga, what are you doing here? You need to get away from all of this and go see Anita." I lightly touch the wound causing the stream of blood. "She can help you heal."

Naga feels useless. Naga wants to get them back for what they did to Eir. Naga wants to fight. His bottom lip protrudes in a pout.

I stroke his face, and he nuzzles into my hand. "Naga, go fix yourself. You need to leave this battle. You can't help like this. You would make me happy if you go to see Anita." I search the sky, looking for Drogon. "I'm surprised Drogon left you here."

Naga shook his head. *No. Drogon didn't leave Naga here. Naga made his way here and was attacked by a spear. The elf dug into Naga's side.*

"I can see that. Where did the dark elf go?"

Naga flicked his nose toward the edge of the boulder. I glance over and find a head sitting by itself, bodiless.

"I guess you taught him. Good job, Naga. You need to rest and heal. After that, we can go and find Eir. Hopefully, she's okay. But you need to be in your top condition to be able to do that."

I didn't even think it was possible for Naga's eyes to look so sad.

"Oh, Naga." I stroke his face some more.

Naga feel so helpless.

"I understand, Naga. I do." I look deep into his eyes. "But you need to look after yourself. Eir needs you, but she needs you to be in your top form."

Naga's deep-blue eyes turn to mine before he slowly nods.

"Are you okay to get to Anita? She will help you."

Naga steps forward and winces. He pauses, and I'm ready to run to his side. *It will take a while, but Naga can do it. Kara go help others. They need your help with this war.*

I touch his front leg. "Take care, Naga. Go and get healed."

Naga limps away, and I can see that his heart is filled with sadness. I want to break. I'm worried about Eir, but I'm still hoping that she is okay. I hold a deep longing for my peaceful friend. She should've been the least-likely target because she's so peaceful and doesn't like to strike first. The last time something terrible happened to Eir, Naga saved her, but this time he couldn't. Nobody could. And then she disappeared. Her body is gone.

With this in mind, I clench my teeth and glance over at the battle. I pull my sword out of its sheath and charge. "For Eir," I cry, swinging the sword the second I reach a dark elf.

Ragnarök will not happen on my watch. As though answering my cry, Elan's roar echoes off the mountains, through the skies, and into the valley below. The einherjar, the Valkyries, and the angels of death scream the war cry with her in unison.

The End

Deceived: Book 10 is released in January, 2020.

ACKNOWLEDGMENTS

I am touched by the enormous amount of support I have received from my immediate family. My husband has been a helpful first reader and at times been a wonderful motivator, with hints of ideas to help me through the blanks. The support from my three sons has also been overwhelming. They have put up with my head being in the clouds, thinking about the next plot twist or story for several years. Along with many hours spent working on my books and keeping in touch with my readers.

A big thank you to my extended family who support me being a book enthusiast.

A huge thank you to my editor, Neila Forssberg., her editing and writing tips, and my Proofreader, Susie D., for picking up the things we missed.

Thank you to all of my readers who have loved my work, and continue to read my stories. I would love for you to share your thoughts in a review on one or all of the following:

Amazon.com

Goodreads

Barnes & Noble

You can follow Katrina Cope at:

https://www.facebook.com/Author.Katrina.Cope

https://twitter.com/Katrina_R_Cope

https://www.goodreads.com/author/show/7265107.Katrina_Cope

https://www.katrinacopebooks.com

http://http://www.amazon.com/Katrina-Cope/e/B00F00JF9M/

BOOKS BY KATRINA COPE

~~~~~

Pre-Teen Books

THE SANCTUM SERIES

JAYDEN'S CYBERMOUNTAIN

SCARLET'S ESCAPE

TAYLOR'S PLIGHT

ERIC & THE BLACK AXES

ADRIANNA'S SURGE

~~~~~

Young Adult Urban Fantasy

AFTERLIFE SERIES

FLEDGLING

THE TAKING

ANGELIC RETRIBUTION

DIVIDED PATHS

Afterlife Novelette

THE GATEKEEPER

~~~~~

Young Adult Urban Paranormal Fantasy

SUPERNATURAL EVOLVEMENT SERIES

(Associated with the Afterlife Series)

WITCH'S LEGACY (#0.5 Prequel)

AALIYAH

~~~~~

Young Adult Fantasy Nordic Myths

VALKYRIE ACADEMY DRAGON ALLIANCE

SERIES

MARKED (Prequel)

CHOSEN

VANISHED

SCORNED

INFLICTED

EMPOWERED

AMBUSHED

WARNED

ABDUCTED

BESIEGED

DECEIVED

DID YOU ENJOY THIS BOOK?
YOU CAN MAKE A BIG DIFFERENCE.

Honest reviews of my books help bring them to the attention of other readers.

If you've enjoyed this book, I'd be grateful if you could spend a few minutes leaving a review (it can be as short as you like).
The review can be left on Amazon and Goodreads.
Thank you very much.

ABOUT THE AUTHOR

Katrina is an author of several Young Adult and Preteen/Middle Grade novels. Each of her released books reaching the top 100 in certain categories on the Amazon's Best Sellers Rank – a few even as high as number one.

She resides in Queensland, Australia. Her three teenage boys and husband for over nineteen years treat her like a princess. Unfortunately though, this princess still has to do domestic chores.

From a very young age, she has been a very creative person and has spent many years travelling the world and observing many different personalities and cultures. Her favourite personalities have been the strange ones, yet the ones under the radar also hold a place in her heart.

During her last extensive travels, she spent 16 nights in a bomb shelter on a Kibbutz 8 kilometers off the Lebanese border. It was to avoid Katyusha bombs that the resident volunteers decided to name her after (she is still trying to work out why).

Katrina's online home is at
www.katrinacopebooks.com

You can connect with Katrina on:

Twitter https://twitter.com/Katrina_R_Cope

Facebook
https://www.facebook.com/Author.Katrina.Cope

Instagram
https://www.instagram.com/katrina_cope_author

Pinterest
https://www.pinterest.com.au/katrinacope56

Email authorkatrinacope@gmail.com